Faber
Stories

Junot Díaz is the author of *Drown*, *The Brief Wondrous Life of Oscar Wao*, which won the National Book Critics Circle Award and the Pulitzer Prize in 2007, and *This is How You Lose Her*. He is the recipient of a PEN/Malamud Award and the Dayton Literary Peace Prize. Born in Santo Domingo, Díaz is a professor at MIT.

Junot Díaz

The
Cheater's
Guide to
Love

Faber
Stories

ff

First published in this edition in 2019
by Faber & Faber Limited
Bloomsbury House
74–77 Great Russell Street
London WC1B 3DA
First published in *This Is How You Lose Her* in 2012

Typeset by Faber & Faber Limited
Printed and bound by CPI Group (UK) Ltd, Croydon, CR0 4YY

All rights reserved
© Junot Díaz, 2012

The right of Junot Díaz to be identified as author of this work
has been asserted in accordance with Section 77 of the Copyright,
Designs and Patents Act 1988

A CIP record for this book
is available from the British Library

ISBN 978–0–571–35599–0

MIX
Paper from
responsible sources
FSC® C020471

10 9 8 7 6 5 4 3 2 1

Year 0

Your girl catches you cheating. (Well, actually she's your fiancée, but hey, in a bit it *so* won't matter.) She could have caught you with one sucia, she could have caught you with two, but as you're a totally batshit cuero who didn't ever empty his e-mail trash can, she caught you with fifty! Sure, over a six-year period, but still. Fifty fucking girls? God*damn*. Maybe if you'd been engaged to a super open-minded blanquita you could have survived it—but you're not engaged to a super open-minded blanquita. Your girl is a bad-ass salcedeña who doesn't believe in open anything; in fact the one thing she warned you about, that she swore she would never forgive, was *cheating*. I'll put a machete in you, she promised. And of course you swore you wouldn't do it. You swore you wouldn't. You swore you wouldn't.

And you did.

She'll stick around for a few months because

you dated for a long long time. Because you went through much together—her father's death, your tenure madness, her bar exam (passed on the third attempt). And because love, real love, is not so easily shed. Over a tortured six-month period you will fly to the DR, to Mexico (for the funeral of a friend), to New Zealand. You will walk the beach where they filmed *The Piano*, something she's always wanted to do, and now, in penitent desperation, you give it to her. She is immensely sad on that beach and she walks up and down the shining sand alone, bare feet in the freezing water, and when you try to hug her she says, *Don't*. She stares at the rocks jutting out of the water, the wind taking her hair straight back. On the ride back to the hotel, up through those wild steeps, you pick up a pair of hitch-hikers, a couple, so mixed it's ridiculous, and so giddy with love that you almost throw them out the car. She says nothing. Later, in the hotel, she will cry.

You try every trick in the book to keep her. You write her letters. You drive her to work. You quote Neruda. You compose a mass e-mail disowning all your sucias. You block their e-mails. You change your phone number. You stop drinking. You stop smoking. You claim you're a sex addict and start attending meetings. You blame your father. You blame your mother. You blame the patriarchy. You blame Santo Domingo. You find a therapist. You cancel your Facebook. You give her the passwords to all your e-mail accounts. You start taking salsa classes like you always swore you would so that the two of you could dance together. You claim that you were sick, you claim that you were weak—It was the book! It was the pressure!—and every hour like clockwork you say that you're so so sorry. You try it all, but one day she will simply sit up in bed and say, *No more*, and, *Ya*, and you will have to move from the Harlem apartment that you two have shared. You consider not going. You consider a squat protest. In fact, you say you won't go. But in the end you do.

For a while you haunt the city, like a two-bit ballplayer dreaming of a call-up. You phone her every day and leave messages which she doesn't answer. You write her long sensitive letters, which

3

she returns unopened. You even show up at her apartment at odd hours and at her job downtown until finally her little sister calls you, the one who was always on your side, and she makes it plain: If you try to contact my sister again she's going to put a restraining order on you.

For some Negroes that wouldn't mean shit.

But you ain't that kind of Negro.

You stop. You move back to Boston. You never see her again.

Year 1

At first you pretend it don't matter. You harbored a lot of grievances against her anyway. Yes you did! She didn't give good head, you hated the fuzz on her cheeks, she never waxed her pussy, she never cleaned up around the apartment, etc. For a few weeks you almost believe it. Of course you go back to smoking, to drinking, you drop the therapist and the sex addict groups and you run around with the sluts like it's the good old days, like nothing has happened.

I'm back, you say to your boys.

Elvis laughs. It's almost like you never left.

You're good for like a week. Then your moods become erratic. One minute you have to stop yourself from jumping in the car and driving to see her and the next you're calling a sucia and saying, You're the one I always wanted. You start losing your temper with friends, with students, with colleagues. You cry every time you hear Monchy and Alexandra, her favorite.

Boston, where you never wanted to live, where you feel you've been exiled to, becomes a serious problem. You have trouble adjusting to it full-time; to its trains that stop running at midnight, to the glumness of its inhabitants, to its startling lack of Sichuan food. Almost on cue a lot of racist shit starts happening. Maybe it was always there, maybe you've become more sensitive after all your time in NYC. White people pull up at traffic lights and scream at you with a hideous rage, like you nearly ran over their mothers. It's fucking scary. Before you can figure out what the fuck is going on they flip you the bird and peel out. It happens again and again. Security follows you in stores and every time you step on Harvard property you're asked for ID. Three times, drunk whitedudes try to pick fights with you in different parts of the city.

You take it all very personally. I hope someone drops a fucking *bomb* on this city, you rant. This is why no people of color want to live here. Why all my black and Latino students leave as soon as they can.

Elvis says nothing. He was born and raised in Jamaica Plain, knows that trying to defend Boston from uncool is like blocking a bullet with a slice of bread. Are you OK? he asks finally.

I'm dandy, you say. Mejor que nunca.

Except you're not. You've lost all the mutual friends you had in NYC (they went to her), your mother won't speak to you after what happened (she liked the fiancée better than she liked you), and you're feeling terribly guilty and terribly alone. You keep writing letters to her, waiting for the day that you can hand them to her. You also keep fucking everything that moves. Thanksgiving you end up having to spend in your apartment because you can't face your mom and the idea of other people's charity makes you furious. The ex, as you're now calling her, always cooked: a turkey, a chicken, a pernil. Set aside all the wings for you. That night you drink yourself into a stupor, spend two days recovering.

You figure that's as bad as it gets. You figure wrong. During finals a depression rolls over you, so profound you doubt there is a name for it. It feels like you're being slowly pincered apart, atom by atom.

You stop hitting the gym or going out for drinks; you stop shaving or washing your clothes; in fact, you stop doing almost everything. Your friends begin to worry about you, and they are not exactly the worrying types. I'm OK, you tell them, but with each passing week the depression darkens. You try to describe it. Like someone flew a plane into your soul. Like someone flew two planes into your soul. Elvis sits shivah with you in the apartment; he pats you on the shoulder, tells you to take it easy. Four years earlier Elvis had a Humvee blow up on him on a highway outside of Baghdad. The burning wreckage pinned him for what felt like a week, so he knows a little about pain. His back and buttocks and right arm so scarred up that even you, Mr. Hard Nose, can't look at them. Breathe, he tells you. You breathe nonstop, like a marathon runner, but it doesn't help. Your little letters become more and more pathetic. *Please*, you write. *Please come back*. You have dreams where she's talking to you like in the old days—in that sweet Spanish of the Cibao, no sign of rage, of disappointment. And then you wake up.

You stop sleeping, and some night when you're drunk and alone you have a wacky impulse to open the window of your fifth-floor apartment and leap down to the street. If it wasn't for a couple of things you probably would have done it, too. But (a) you ain't the killing-yourself type; (b) your boy Elvis keeps a strong eye on you—he's over all the time, stands by the window as if he knows what you're thinking. And (c) you have this ridiculous hope that maybe one day she will forgive you.

She doesn't.

Year 2

You make it through both semesters, barely. It really is a long stretch of shit and then finally the madness begins to recede. It's like waking up from the worst fever of your life. You ain't your old self (har-har!) but you can stand near windows without being overcome by strange urges, and that's a start. Unfortunately, you've put on forty-five pounds. You don't know how it happened but it happened. Only one pair of your jeans fits anymore, and none of your suits. You put away all the old pictures of her, say goodbye to her Wonder Woman features. You go to the barber, shave your head for the first time in forever and cut off your beard.

You done? Elvis asks.

I'm done.

A white grandma screams at you at a traffic light and you close your eyes until she goes away.

Find yourself another girl, Elvis advises. He's holding his daughter lightly. Clavo saca clavo.

Nothing sacas nothing, you reply. No one will ever be like her.

OK. But find yourself a girl anyway.

His daughter was born that February. If she had been a boy Elvis was going to name him Iraq, his wife told you.

I'm sure he was kidding.

She looked out to where he was working on his truck. I don't think so.

He puts his daughter in your arms. Find yourself a good Dominican girl, he says.

You hold the baby uncertainly. Your ex never wanted kids but toward the end she made you get a sperm test, just in case she decided last minute to change her mind. You put your lips against the baby's stomach and blow. Do they even exist?

You had one, didn't you?

That you did.

You clean up your act. You cut it out with all the old sucias, even the long-term Iranian girl you'd boned the entire time you were with the fiancée. You want to turn over a new leaf. Takes you a bit—after all, old sluts are the hardest habit to ditch—but you finally break clear and when you do you feel lighter. I should have done this years ago, you declare, and your girl Arlenny, who never ever messed with you (Thank God, she mutters) rolls her eyes. You wait, what, a week for the bad energy to dissipate and then you start dating. Like a normal person, you tell Elvis. Without any lies. Elvis says nothing, only smiles.

At first it's OK: you get numbers but nothing you would take home to the fam. But after the early rush, it all dries up. It ain't just a dry spell; it's fucking Arrakeen. You're out all the time but no one seems to be biting. Not even the chicks who swear they *love Latin guys*, and one girl, when you tell her you are Dominican, actually says, Hell no and runs full-tilt toward the door. Seriously? you say. You begin to wonder if there is some secret mark on your forehead. If some of these bitches *know*.

Be patient, Elvis urges. He's working for this ghetto-ass landlord and starts taking you with him on collection day. It turns out you're awesome backup. Deadbeats catch one peep of your dismal grill and cough up their debts with a quickness.

One month, two month, three month and then some hope. Her name is Noemi, Dominican from Baní—in Massachusetts it seems all the domos are from Baní—and you meet at Sofia's in the last months before it closes, fucking up the Latino community of New England forever. She ain't half your ex but she ain't bad either. She's a nurse, and when Elvis complains about his back, she starts listing all the shit it might be. She's a big girl and got skin like you wouldn't believe and best of all she doesn't privar at all; actually seems *nice*. She smiles often and whenever she's nervous she says, Tell me something. Minuses: she's always working and she has a four-year-old named Justin. She shows you pictures; kid looks like he'll be dropping an album if she's not careful. She had him with a banilejo who had four other kids with four other women. And you thought this guy was a good idea for what reason? you say. I was stupid, she admits. Where did you meet him? Same place I met you, she says. Out.

Normally that would be a no-go, but Noemi is not only nice, she's also kinda fly. One of those hot moms and you're excited for the first time in over a year. Even standing next to her while a hostess looks for menus gives you an erection.

Sunday is her one day off—the Five-Baby Father watches Justin that day, or better said, he and his new girlfriend watch Justin that day. You and Noemi fall into a little pattern: on Saturday you take her out to dinner—she doesn't eat anything remotely adventurous, so it's always Italian—and then she stays the night.

How sweet was that toto? Elvis asks after the first sleepover.

Not sweet at all, because Noemi doesn't give it to you! Three Saturdays in a row she sleeps over, and three Saturdays in a row nada. A little kissing, a little feeling up, but nothing beyond that. She brings her own pillow, one of those expensive foam ones, and her own toothbrush, and she takes it all with her Sunday morning. Kisses you at the door as she leaves; it all feels too chaste to you, too lacking in promise.

No toto? Elvis looks a little shocked.

No toto, you confirm. What am I, in sixth grade?

You know you should be patient. You know she's just testing your ass. She's probably had a lot of bad experiences with the hit-and-run types. Case in point—Justin's dad. But it galls you that she gave it up to some thug with no job, no education, no nothing, but she's making you jump through hoops of fire. In fact, it infuriates you.

Are we going to see each other? she asks on week four, and you almost say yes but then your idiocy gets the best of you.

It depends, you say.

On what? She is instantly guarded and that adds to your irritation. Where was that guard when she let the banilejo fuck her without a condom?

On whether you're planning to give me ass anytime soon.

Oh classiness. You know as soon as you say it that you just buried yourself.

Noemi is silent. Then she says: Let me get off this phone before I say something you won't like.

This is your last chance, but instead of begging for mercy you bark: *Fine*.

Within an hour she has deleted you from Facebook. You send one exploratory text to her but it is never answered.

Years later you will see her in Dudley Square but she will pretend not to recognize you, and you won't force the issue.

Nicely done, Elvis says. Bravo.

You two are watching his daughter knock around the playground near Columbia Terrace. He tries to be reassuring. She had a kid. That probably wasn't for you.

Probably not.

Even these little breakups suck because they send you right back to thinking about the ex. Right back into the depression. This time you spend six months wallowing in it before you come back to the world.

After you pull yourself back together you tell Elvis: I think I need a break from the bitches.

What are you going to do?

Focus on me for a while.

That's a good idea, says his wife. Besides it only happens when you're not looking for it.

That's what everybody claims. Easier to say that than This shit sucks.

This shit sucks, Elvis says. Does that help?

Not really.

On the walk home a Jeep roars past; the driver calls you a *fucking towelhead*. One of the ex-sucias publishes a poem about you online. It's called "El Puto."

Year 3

You take your break. You try to get back to your work, to your writing. You start three novels: one about a pelotero, one about a narco and one about a bachatero—all of them suck pipe. You get serious about classes and for your health you take up running. You used to run in the old days and you figure you need something to keep you out of your head. You must have needed it bad, because once you get into the swing of it you start running four five six times a week. It's your new addiction. You run in the morning and you run late at night when there's no one on the paths next to the Charles. You run so hard that your heart feels like it's going to seize. When winter rolls in, there's a part of you that fears you'll fold—Boston winters are on some terrorism shit—but you need the activity more than anything so you keep at it even as the trees are stripped of their foliage and the paths empty out and the frost reaches into your bones. Soon it's only you and a couple of other lunatics. Your body changes, of course. You lose all that drinking and smoking chub and your legs look like they belong to someone else. Every time you think about the ex, every time the loneliness rears up in you like a seething, burning continent, you tie on your shoes and hit the paths and that helps; it really does.

By winter's end you've gotten to know all the morning regulars and there's even this one girl who inspires in you some hope. You pass each other a couple of times a week and she's a pleasure to watch, a gazelle really—what economy, what gait, and what an amazing fucking cuerpazo. She has Latin features but your radar has been off a while and she could just as likely be a morena as anything. She always smiles at you as you pass. You consider flopping in front of her—My leg! My leg!—but that seems incredibly cursí. You keep hoping you'll bump into her around town.

The running is going splendid and then six months in you feel a pain in your right foot. Along the inside arch, a burning that doesn't subside after a few days' rest. Soon you're hobbling even when you're not running. You drop in on emergency care and the RN pushes with his thumb, watches you writhe, and announces you have plantar fasciitis.

You have no idea what that is. When can I run again?

He gives you a pamphlet. Sometimes it takes a month. Sometimes six months. Sometimes a year. He pauses. Sometimes longer.

That makes you so sad you go home and lie in bed in the dark. You're afraid. I don't want to go back down the hole, you tell Elvis. Then don't, he says. Like a hardhead you keep trying to run but the pain sharpens. Finally, you give up. You put away the shoes. You sleep in. When you see other people hitting the paths, you turn away. You find yourself crying in front of sporting goods stores. Out of nowhere you call the ex, but of course she doesn't pick up. The fact that she hasn't changed her number gives you some strange hope, even though you've heard she's dating somebody. Word on the street is that the dude is super good to her.

Elvis encourages you to try yoga, the half-Bikram kind they teach in Central Square. Mad fucking ho's in there, he says. I'm talking ho's by the ton. While you're not exactly feeling the ho's right now, you don't want to lose all the conditioning you've built up, so you give it a shot. The namaste bullshit you could do without, but you fall into it and soon you're pulling vinyasas with the best of them. Elvis was certainly right. There are mad ho's, all with their asses in the air, but none of them catch your eye. One miniature blanquita does try to chat you up. She seems impressed that of all the guys in class you alone never take off your shirt, but you skitter away from her cornpoke grin. What the hell are you going to do with a blanquita?

Bone the shit out of her, Elvis offers.

Bust a nut in her mouth, your boy Darnell seconds.

Give her a chance, Arlenny proposes.

But you don't do any of it. At the end of the sessions you move away quickly to wipe down your mat and she takes the hint. She doesn't mess with you again, though sometimes during practice she watches you with longing.

You actually become pretty obsessed with yoga and soon you're taking your mat with you wherever you go. You no longer have fantasies that the ex will be waiting for you in front of your apartment, though every now and then you still call her and let the phone ring to the in-box.

You finally start work on your eighties apocalypse novel—"finally starting" means you write one paragraph—and in a flush of confidence you start messing with this young morena from the Harvard Law School that you meet at the Enormous Room. She's half your age, one of those super geniuses who finished undergrad when she was nineteen and is seriously lovely. Elvis and Darnell approve. Aces, they say. Arlenny demurs. She's really young, no? Yes, she's really young and you fuck a whole lot and during the act the two of you cling to each other for dear life but afterward you peel away like you're ashamed of yourselves. Most of the time you suspect she feels sorry for you. She says she likes your mind, but considering that she's smarter than you, that seems doubtful. What she does appear to like is your body, can't keep her hands off it. I should get back to ballet, she says while undressing you. Then you'd lose your thick, you note, and she laughs. I know, that's the dilemma.

It's all going swell, going marvelous, and then in the middle of a sun salutation you feel a shift in your lower back and *pau*—it's like a sudden power failure. You lose all strength, have to lie down. Yes, urges the instructor, rest if you have to. When the class is over you need help from the little whitegirl to rise to your feet. Do you want me to take you somewhere? she asks but you shake your head. The walk back to your apartment is some Bataan-type shit. At the Plough and Stars you fall against a stop sign and call Elvis on your cell.

He arrives in a flash with a hottie in tow. She's a straight-up Cambridge Cape Verdean. The two of them look like they've just been fucking. Who's that? you ask and he shakes his head. Drags you into emergency care. By the time the doctor appears you're crabbed over like an old man.

It appears to be a ruptured disc, she announces.

Yay, you say.

You're in bed for a solid two weeks. Elvis brings you food and sits with you while you eat. He talks about the Cape Verdean girl. She's got like the perfect pussy, he says. It's like putting your dick in a hot mango.

You listen for a bit and then you say: Just don't end up like me.

Elvis grins. Shit, no one could ever end up like you, Yunior. You're a DR original.

His daughter throws your books onto the floor. You don't care. Maybe it will encourage her to read, you say.

So now it's your feet, your back, and your heart. You can't run, you can't do yoga. You try riding a bike, thinking you'll turn into an Armstrong, but it kills your back. So you stick to walking. You do it one hour each morning and one hour each night. There is no rush to the head, no tearing up your lungs, no massive shock to your system, but it's better than nothing.

A month later the law student leaves you for one of her classmates, tells you that it was great but she has to start being realistic. Translation: I got to stop fucking with old dudes. Later you see her with said classmate on the Yard. He's even lighter than you but he still looks unquestionably black. He's also like nine feet tall and put together like an anatomy primer. They are walking hand in hand and she looks so very happy that you try to find the space in your heart not to begrudge her. Two seconds later, security approaches you and asks for ID. The next day a whitekid on a bike throws a can of Diet Coke at you.

Classes start and by then the squares on your abdomen have been reabsorbed, like tiny islands in a rising sea of lard. You scan the incoming junior faculty for a possible, but there's nothing. You watch a lot of TV. Sometimes Elvis joins you since his wife doesn't allow him to smoke weed in the house. He's taken up yoga now, having seen what it did for you. Lots of ho's, too, he says, grinning. You want not to hate him.

What happened to the Cape Verdean girl?

What Cape Verdean girl? he says dryly.

You make little advances. You start doing push-ups and pull-ups and even some of your old yoga moves, but very carefully. You have dinner with a couple of girls. One of them is married and hot for days in the late-thirties Dominican middle-class woman sort of way. You can tell she's contemplating sleeping with you and the whole time you're eating your short ribs you feel like you're on the dock. In Santo Domingo I'd never be able to meet you like this, she says with great generosity. Almost all her conversations start with In Santo Domingo. She's doing a year at the business school and for how much she gushes about Boston you can tell she misses the DR, would never live anywhere else.

Boston is really racist, you offer by way of orientation.

She looks at you like you're crazy. Boston isn't racist, she says. She also scoffs at the idea of racism in Santo Domingo.

So Dominicans *love* Haitians now?

26

That's not about race. She pronounces every syllable. That's about *nationality*.

Of course you end up in bed and it ain't bad except for the fact that she never never comes and she spends a lot of time complaining about her husband. She takes, if you get my meaning, and soon you are squiring her around the city and beyond: to Salem on Halloween and one weekend to the Cape. No one ever pulls you over when you are with her or asks you for ID. Everywhere you two go she shoots fotos but never any of you. She writes her kids postcards while you're in bed.

At the end of the semester she returns home. My home, not your home, she says tetchily. She's always trying to prove you're not Dominican. If I'm not Dominican then no one is, you shoot back, but she laughs at that. Say that in Spanish, she challenges and of course you can't. Last day you drive her to the airport and there is no crushing *Casablanca* kiss, just a smile and a little gay-ass hug and her fake breasts push against you like something irrevocable. Write, you tell her, and she says, Por supuesto, and of course neither of you do. You eventually erase her contact info from your phone but not the pictures you took of her in bed while she was naked and asleep, never those.

Year 4

Wedding invitations from the ex-sucias start to arrive in the mail. You have no idea how to explain this berserkería. What the fuck, you say. You reach out to Arlenny for insight. She turns over the cards. I guess it's what Oates said: Revenge is living well, without you. Fuck Hall and Oates, Elvis says. These bitches think we're bitches. They think we're gonna give a shit about vaina like this. He peers at the invite. Is it me or does every Asian girl on the planet marry a white guy? Is it written on the genes or something?

That year your arms and legs begin to give you trouble, occasionally going numb, flickering in and out like a brownout back on the Island. It is a strange pins-and-needles feeling. What the fuck is this? you wonder. I hope I'm not dying. You're probably working out too hard, Elvis says. But I'm not really working out at all, you protest. Probably just stress, the nurse at emergency care tells you. You hope so, flexing your hands, worrying. You really do hope so.

March you fly out to the Bay to deliver a lecture, which does not go well; almost no one shows up beyond those who were forced to by their professors. Afterward you head alone to K-town and gorge on kalbi until you're ready to burst. You drive around for a couple of hours, just to get a feel of the city. You have a couple of friends in town but you don't call them because you know they'll only want to talk to you about old times, about the ex. You have a sucia in town too and in the end you call her but when she hears your name she hangs up on your ass.

When you return to Boston the law student is waiting for you in the lobby of your building. You are surprised and excited and a little wary. What's up?

It's like bad television. You notice that she has lined up three suitcases in the foyer. And on closer inspection her ridiculously Persian-looking eyes are red from crying, her mascara freshly applied.

I'm pregnant, she says.

At first you don't register it. You joke: And?

You *asshole*. She starts crying. It's probably your stupid fucking kid.

There are surprises and there are surprises and then there is this.

You don't know what to say or how to act, so you bring her upstairs. You lug up the suitcases despite your back, despite your foot, despite your flickering arms. She says nothing, just hugs her pillow to her Howard sweater. She is a Southern girl with supremely straight posture and when she sits down you feel as if she's preparing to interview you. After serving her tea you ask: Are you keeping it?

Of course I'm keeping *it*.

What about Kimathi?

She doesn't get it. Who?

Your Kenyan. You can't bring yourself to say *boyfriend*.

He threw me out. He knows it's not his. She picks at something on her sweater. I'm going to unpack, OK? You nod and watch her. She is an exceptionally beautiful girl. You think of that old saying *Show me a beautiful girl and I'll show you someone who is tired of fucking her*. You doubt you would have ever tired of her, though.

But it could be his, right?

It's yours, OK? she cries. I know you don't want it to be yours but it's yours.

You are surprised at how hollowed out you feel. You don't know if you should show enthusiasm or support. You run your hand over the thinning stubble on your head.

I need to stay here, she tells you later, after the two of you fumble through an awkward fuck. I have nowhere to go. I can't go back to my family.

When you tell Elvis the whole story you expect him to flip out, to order you to kick her out. You fear his reaction because you know you don't have the heart to kick her out.

But Elvis doesn't flip. He slaps you on the back, beams delightedly. That's great, cuz.

What do you mean, That's great?

You're going to be a father. You're going to have a son.

A son? What are you talking about? There's not even proof that it's mine.

Elvis is not listening. He's smiling at some inner thought. He checks to make sure the wife is not anywhere in earshot. Remember the last time we went to the DR?

Of course you do. Three years ago. Everybody had a blast except for you. You were in the middle of the great downturn, which meant you spent most of your time alone, floating on your back in the ocean or getting drunk at the bar or walking the beach in the early morning before anybody was up.

What about it?

Well, I got a girl pregnant while we were down there.

Are you fucking kidding me?

He nods.

Pregnant?

He nods again.

Did she have it?

He rummages through his cell phone. Shows you

a picture of a perfect little boy with the most Dominican little face you ever done saw.

That's my son, Elvis says proudly. Elvis Xavier Junior.

Dude, are you fucking *serious* with this? If your wife finds—

He bridles. She ain't going to find out.

You sit on it for a bit. You're posted up behind his house, near Central Square. In summer these blocks are ill with activity but today you can actually hear a jay chivvying some other birds.

Babies are fucking expensive. Elvis punches you in the arm. So just get ready, buster, to be broke as a joke.

Back at the apartment the law student has taken over two of your closets and almost your entire sink and most crucially she has laid claim to the bed. She has put a pillow and a sheet on the couch. For you.

What, am I not allowed to share the bed with you?

I don't think it's good for me, she says. It would be too stressful. I don't want to miscarry.

Hard to argue against that. Your back doesn't take to the couch at all, so now you wake up in the morning in more pain than ever.

Only a bitch of color comes to Harvard to get pregnant. White women don't do that. Asian women don't do that. Only fucking black and Latina women. Why go to all the trouble to get into Harvard just to get knocked up? You could have stayed on the block and done that shit.

This is what you write in your journal. The next day when you return from classes the law student throws the notebook in your face. I fucking *hate you*, she wails. I *hope* it's not yours. I *hope* it *is* yours and it's born *retarded*.

How can you say that? you demand. How can you say something like that?

She walks to the kitchen and starts to pour herself a shot and you find yourself pulling the bottle out of her hand and pouring its contents into the sink. This is ridiculous, you say. More bad TV.

She doesn't speak to you again for two whole fucking weeks. You spend as much time as you can either at your office or over at Elvis's house. Whenever you enter a room she snaps shut her laptop. I'm not fucking snooping, you say. But she waits for you to move on before she returns to typing whatever she was typing.

You can't throw out your baby's mom, Elvis reminds you. It would fuck that kid up for life. Plus, it's bad karma. Just wait till the baby comes. She'll fucking straighten out.

A month passes, two months pass. You're afraid to tell anybody else, to share the—what? Good news? Arlenny you know would march right in and boot her ass out on the street. Your back is agony and the numbness in your arms is starting to become pretty steady. In the shower, the only place in the apartment you can be alone, you whisper to yourself: *Hell, Netley. We're in Hell.*

Later it will all come back to you as a terrible fever dream but at the time it moved so very slowly, felt so very concrete. You take her to her appointments. You help her with the vitamins and shit. You pay for almost everything. She is not speaking to her mother so all she has are two friends who are in the apartment almost as much as you are. They are all part of the Biracial Identity Crisis Support Group and look at you with little warmth. You wait for her to melt, but she keeps her distance. Some days while she is sleeping and you are trying to work you allow yourself the indulgence of wondering what kind of child you will have. Whether it will be a boy or a girl, smart or withdrawn. Like you or like her.

Have you thought up any names? Elvis's wife asks.

Not yet.

Taína for a girl, she suggests. And Elvis for a boy. She throws a taunting glance at her husband and laughs.

I like my name, Elvis says. I would give it to a boy.

Over my dead body, his wife says. And besides, this oven is closed for business.

At night while you're trying to sleep you see the glow of her computer through the open door of the

37

bedroom, hear her fingers on the keyboard.

Do you need anything?

I'm fine, thank you.

You come to the door a few times and watch her, wanting to be called in, but she always glares and asks you, What the fuck do you want?

Just checking.

Five month, six month, seventh month. You are in class teaching Intro to Fiction when you get a text from one of her girlfriends saying she has gone into labor, six weeks early. All sorts of terrible fears race around inside of you. You keep trying her cell phone but she doesn't answer. You call Elvis but he doesn't answer either, so you drive over to the hospital by yourself.

Are you the father? the woman at the desk asks.

I am, you say diffidently.

You are led around the corridors and finally given some scrubs and told to wash your hands and given instructions where you should stand and warned about the procedure but as soon as you walk into the birthing room the law student shrieks: *I don't want him in here. I don't want him in here. He's not the father.*

You didn't think anything could hurt so bad. Her two girlfriends rush at you but you have already exited. You saw her thin ashy legs and the doctor's back and little else. You're glad you didn't see anything more. You would have felt like you'd violated her safety or something. You take off the scrubs; you wait around for a bit and then you realize what you're doing and finally you drive home.

You don't hear from her but from her girlfriend, the same one who texted you about the labor. I'll come pick up her bags, OK? When she arrives, she glances around the apartment warily. You're not going to go psycho on me, are you?

No, I'm not. After a pause you demand: Why would you say that? I've never hurt a woman in my life. Then you realize how you sound—like a dude who hurts women all the time. Everything goes back into the three suitcases and then you help her wrestle them down to her SUV.

You must be relieved, she says.

You don't answer.

And that's the end of it. Later you hear that the Kenyan visited her in the hospital, and when he saw the baby a teary reconciliation occurred, all was forgiven.

That was your mistake, Elvis said. You should have had a baby with that ex of yours. Then she wouldn't have left you.

She would have left you, Arlenny says. Believe it.

The rest of the semester ends up being a super-duper clusterfuck. Lowest evaluations in your six years as a professor. Your only student of color for that semester writes: He claims that we don't know anything but doesn't show us any way to address these deficiencies. One night you call your ex and when the voice mail clicks on you say: We should have had a kid. And then you hang up, ashamed. Why did you say that? you ask yourself. Now she'll definitely never speak to you again.

I don't think the phone call is the problem, Arlenny says.

Check it out. Elvis produces a picture of Elvis Jr. holding a bat. This kid is going to be a monster.

On winter break you fly to the DR with Elvis. What the hell else are you going to do? You ain't got shit going on, outside of waving your arms around every time they go numb.

Elvis is beyond excited. He has three suitcases of shit for the boy, including his first glove, his first ball, his first Bosox jersey. About eighty kilos of clothes and shit for the baby mama. Hid them all in your apartment, too. You are at his house when he bids his wife and mother-in-law and daughter goodbye. His daughter doesn't seem to understand what's happening but when the door shuts she lets out a wail that coils about you like constantine wire. Elvis stays cool as fuck. This used to be me, you're thinking. Me me me.

Of course you look for her on the flight. You can't help yourself.

You assume that the baby mama will live somewhere poor like Capotillo or Los Alcarrizos but you didn't imagine she would live in the Nadalands.

You've been to the Nadalands a couple of times before; shit, your family came up out of those spaces. Squatter chawls where there are no roads, no lights, no running water, no grid, no anything, where everybody's slapdash house is on top of everybody else's, where it's all mud and shanties and motos and grind and thin smiling motherfuckers everywhere without end, like falling off the rim of civilization. You have to leave the rental jípeta on the last bit of paved road and jump on the back of motoconchos with all the luggage balanced on your backs. Nobody stares because those ain't real loads you're carrying: You've seen a single moto carry a family of five and their pig.

You finally pull up to a tiny little house and out comes Baby Mama—cue happy homecoming. You wish you could say you remember Baby Mama from that long-ago trip, but you do not. She is tall and very thick, exactly how Elvis always likes them. She is no older than twenty-one, twenty-two, with an irresistible Georgina Duluc smile, and when she sees you she gives you a huge abrazo. So the padrino finally decides to visit, she declaims in one of those loud ronca campesina voices. You also meet her mother, her grandmother, her brother, her sister, her three uncles. Seems like everybody is missing teeth.

Elvis picks up the boy. Mi hijo, he sings. Mi hijo.

The boy starts crying.

Baby Mama's place is barely two rooms, one bed, one chair, a little table, a single bulb overhead. More mosquitoes than a refugee camp. Raw sewage in the back. You look at Elvis like what the fuck. The few family fotos hanging on the walls are water-stained. When it rains—Baby Mama lifts up her hands—everything goes.

Don't worry, Elvis says, I'm moving them out this month, if I can get the loot together.

The happy couple leaves you with the family and Elvis Jr. while they visit various negocios to settle accounts and to pick up some necessaries. Baby Mama also wants to show off Elvis, natch.

You sit on a plastic chair in front of the house with the kid in your lap. The neighbors admire you with cheerful avidity. A domino game breaks out and you team up with Baby Mama's brooding brother. Takes him less than five seconds to talk you into ordering a couple of grandes and a bottle of Brugal from the nearby colmado. Also three boxes of cigarettes, a tube of salami, and some cough syrup for a neighbor lady with a congested daughter. Ta muy mal, she says. Of course everybody has a sister or a prima they want you to meet. Que tan mas buena que el Diablo, they guarantee. You all barely finish the first bottle of romo before some of the sisters and primas actually start coming around. They look rough but you got to give it to them for trying. You invite them all to sit down, order more beer and some bad pica pollo.

Just let me know which one you like, a neighbor whispers, and I'll make it happen.

Elvis Jr. watches you with considerable gravitas. He is a piercingly cute carajito. He has all these mosquito bites on his legs and an old scab on his head no one can explain to you. You are suddenly overcome with the urge to cover him with your arms, with your whole body.

Later, Elvis Sr. fills you in on the Plan. I'll bring him over to the States in a few years. I'll tell the wife he was an accident, a one-time thing when I was drunk and I didn't find out about it until now.

And that's going to work?

It will work out, he says testily.

Bro, your wife ain't going to buy that.

And what the fuck do you know? Elvis says. It ain't like your shit ever works.

Can't argue with that. By this point your arms are killing you so you pick up the boy in order to put circulation back in them. You look into his eyes. He looks into yours. He seems preternaturally sapient. MIT-bound, you say, while you nuzzle his pepper-corn hair. He starts to bawl then and you put him down, watch him run around a while.

That's more or less when you know.

The second story of the house is unfinished, rebar poking out of the cinderblock like horrible gnarled follicles, and you and Elvis stand up there and drink beers and stare out beyond the edge of the city, beyond the vast radio dish antennas in the distance, out toward the mountains of the Cibao, the Cordillera Central, where your father was born and where your ex's whole family is from. It's breathtaking.

He's not yours, you tell Elvis.

What are you talking about?

The boy is not yours.

Don't be a jerk. That kid looks just like me.

Elvis. You put your hand on his arm. You look straight into the center of his eyes. Cut the crap.

A long silence. But he looks like me.

Bro, he so doesn't look like you.

The next day you two load up the boy and drive back into the city, back into Gazcue. You literally have to beat the family off to keep them from coming with you. Before you go one of the uncles pulls you aside. You really should bring these people a refrigerator. Then the brother pulls you aside. And a TV. And then the mother pulls you aside. A hot comb too.

Traffic back into the center is Gaza Strip crazy and there seems to be a crash every five hundred meters and Elvis keeps threatening to turn around. You ignore him. You stare at the slurry of broken concrete, the sellers with all the crap of the earth slung over their shoulders, the dust-covered palms. The boy holds on to you tightly. There is no significance in this, you tell yourself. It's a Moro-type reflex, nothing more.

Don't make me do this, Yunior, Elvis pleads.

You insist. You have to, E. You know you can't live a lie. It won't be good for the boy, it won't be good for you. Don't you think it's better to know?

But I always wanted a boy, he says. My whole life that's all I wanted. When I got in that shit in Iraq I kept thinking, Please God let me live just long enough to have a son, please, and then you can kill me dead right after. And look, He gave him to me, didn't He? He gave him to me.

The clinic is in one of those houses they built in the International Style during the time of Trujillo. The two of you stand at the front desk. You are holding the boy's hand. The boy is staring at you with lapidary intensity. The mud is waiting. The mosquito bites are waiting. The Nada is waiting.

Go on, you tell Elvis.

In all honesty you figure he won't do it, that this is where it will end. He'll take the boy and turn around and go back to the jípeta. But he carries the little guy into a room where they swab both their mouths and it's done.

You ask: How long will it take for the results?

Four weeks, the technician tells you.

That long?

She shrugs. Welcome to Santo Domingo.

Year 5

You figure that's the last you'll hear about it, that no matter what, the results will change nothing. But four weeks after the trip, Elvis informs you that the test is negative. Fuck, he says bitterly, fuck fuck fuck. And then he cuts off all contact with the kid and the mother. Changes his cell phone number and e-mail account. I told the bitch not to call me again. There is some shit that can't be forgiven.

Of course you feel terrible. You think about the way the boy looked at you. Let me have her number at least, you say. You figure you can throw her a little cash every month but he won't have it. Fuck that lying bitch.

You reckon he must have known, somewhere inside, maybe even wanted you to blow it all up, but you let it be, don't explore it. He's going to yoga five times a week now, is in the best shape of his life, while you on the other hand have to buy bigger jeans again. When you walk into Elvis's now, his daughter rushes you, calls you Tío Junji. It's your Korean name, Elvis teases.

With him it's like nothing happened. You wish you could be as phlegmatic.

Do you ever think about them?

He shakes his head. Never will either.

The numbness in the arms and legs increases. You return to your doctors and they ship you over to a neurologist who sends you out for an MRI. Looks like you have stenosis all down your spine, the doctor reports, impressed.

Is it bad?

It isn't great. Did you used to do a lot of heavy manual labor?

Besides delivering pool tables, you mean?

That would do it. The doctor squints at the MRI. Let's try some physical therapy. If that doesn't work we'll talk about other options.

Like?

He steeples his fingers contemplatively. Surgery.

From there what little life you got goes south. A student complains to the school that you curse too much. You have to have a sit-down with the dean, who more or less tells you to watch your shit. You get pulled over by the cops three weekends in a row. One time they sit you out on the curb and you watch as all the other whips sail past, passengers ogling you as they go. On the T you swear you peep her in the rush-hour mix and for a second your knees buckle but it turns out to be just another Latina mujerón in a tailored suit.

Of course you dream about her. You are in New Zealand or in Santo Domingo or improbably back in college, in the dorms. You want her to say your name, to touch you, but she doesn't. She just shakes her head.

Ya.

You want to move on, to exorcise shit, so you find a new apartment on the other side of the square that has a view of Harvard skyline. All those amazing steeples, including your favorite, the gray dagger of the Old Cambridge Baptist Church. In the first days of your tenancy an eagle lands in the dead tree right outside your fifth-story window. Looks you in the eye. This seems to you like a good sign.

A month later the law student sends you an invitation to her wedding in Kenya. There's a foto and the two of them are dressed in what you assume is traditional Kenyan jumpoffs. She looks very thin, and she's wearing a lot of makeup. You expect a note, some mention of what you did for her, but there is nothing. Even the address was typed on a computer.

Maybe it's a mistake, you say.

It wasn't a mistake, Arlenny assures you.

Elvis tears the invite up, throws it out the truck window. Fuck that bitch. Fuck all bitches.

You manage to save a tiny piece of the foto. It's of her hand.

You work harder than you've ever worked at everything—the teaching, your physical therapy, your regular therapy, your reading, your walking. You keep waiting for the heaviness to leave you. You keep waiting for the moment you never think about the ex again. It doesn't come.

You ask everybody you know: How long does it usually take to get over it?

There are many formulas. One year for every year you dated. Two years for every year you dated. It's just a matter of willpower: The day you decide it's over, it's over. You never get over it.

One night that winter you go out with all the boys to a ghetto-ass Latin club in Mattapan Square. Murder-fucking-pan. Outside it's close to zero, but inside it's so hot that everybody's stripped down to their T-shirts and the funk is as thick as a fro. There's a girl who keeps bumping into you. You say to her Pero mi amor, ya. And she says: Ya yourself. She's Dominican and lithe and super tall. I could never date anyone as short as you, she informs you very early on in your conversations. But she gives you her number at the end of the night. All evening, Elvis sits at the bar quietly, drinking shot after shot of Rémy. The week before, he took a quick solo trip to the DR, a ghost recon. Didn't tell you about it until after. He tried looking for the mom and Elvis Jr. but they had moved and no one knew where they were. None of the numbers he had for her worked. I hope they turn up, he says.

I hope so, too.

You take the longest walks. Every ten minutes you drop and do squats or push-ups. It's not running, but it raises your heart rate, better than nothing. Afterward you are in so much nerve pain that you can barely move.

Some nights you have *Neuromancer* dreams where you see the ex and the boy and another figure, familiar, waving at you in the distance. *Somewhere, very close, the laugh that wasn't laughter.*

And finally, when you feel like you can do so without blowing into burning atoms, you open a folder you have kept hidden under your bed. The Doomsday Book. Copies of all the e-mails and fotos from the cheating days, the ones the ex found and compiled and mailed to you a month after she ended it. *Dear Yunior, for your next book.* Probably the last time she wrote your name.

You read the whole thing cover to cover (yes, she put covers on it). You are surprised at what a fucking chickenshit coward you are. It kills you to admit it but it's true. You are astounded by the depths of your mendacity. When you finish the Book a second time you say the truth: You did the right thing, negra. You did the right thing.

She's right; this would make a killer book, Elvis says. The two of you have been pulled over by a cop and are waiting for Officer Dickhead to finish running your license. Elvis holds up one of the fotos.

She's Colombian, you say.

He whistles. Que viva Colombia. Hands you back the Book. You really should write the cheater's guide to love.

You think?

I do.

It takes a while. You see the tall girl. You go to more doctors. You celebrate Arlenny's Ph.D. defense. And then one June night you scribble the ex's name and: *The half-life of love is forever.*

You bust out a couple more things. Then you put your head down.

The next day you look at the new pages. For once

you don't want to burn them or give up writing forever.

It's a start, you say to the room.

That's about it. In the months that follow you
bend to the work, because it feels like hope, like
grace—and because you know in your lying cheater's heart that sometimes a start is all we ever get.